Twelfth Night

Based on the play by
William Shakespeare

Retold by Rosie Dickins
Illustrated by Christa Unzner

Reading consultant: Alison Kelly
Roehampton University

❋ The characters ❋

Viola, a young
noblewoman

A sea captain

Sebastian,
Viola's twin
brother

Antonio,
a sailor

Duke Orsino,
ruler of Illyria

Lady Olivia

Malvolio,
Olivia's steward

Sir Toby Belch,
Olivia's uncle

Maria,
Olivia's maid

Sir Andrew Aguecheek,
Sir Toby's friend

Feste,
Olivia's jester

✳ About the story ✳

This story is based on a famous play written by
William Shakespeare 400 years ago. Back then,
people used to celebrate Christmas over twelve
days, finishing with a feast on the twelfth night.
This play would have been staged at that feast.
A love story full of comic twists and turns,
it was the perfect entertainment.

*When you see lines written like this, it
means they are Shakespeare's original words.*

✳ Contents ✳

Chapter 1

Shipwreck

Viola struggled ashore, her dress soaking. All around were breaking waves and broken bits of wood – the remains of the ship she and her brother had been on.

"Sebastian," she called
desperately. But her beloved twin
did not answer.

"He's not here," came a gruff
voice. It was the ship's captain. "But
I saw him clinging to the wreckage,
so he may have survived."

Viola blinked back her tears.
"Where are we?" she asked.

"Illyria," replied the captain.
"Duke Orsino's country."

"What can I do now?" wondered
Viola. "Perhaps the duke will give
me a job. But he's more likely to
hire a man... I know, I'll dress up
as a boy and call myself Cesario."

With the captain's help, she was
soon on her way.

At his palace, Duke Orsino
was listening to love songs and
dreaming about Lady Olivia. He
was hopelessly in love with her –
but she had refused to see him since
her brother, the count, had died.

"What a heart," thought the duke, "to love a brother so much... Oh, if I could only make her love me! I need a messenger," he decided, "someone she won't refuse to see."

Just then, Viola came in, dressed as Cesario, and asked for a job. Orsino took one look at 'his' friendly face and hired 'him' on the spot.

Orsino spent the next three days telling his new servant Cesario all about Olivia, and how much he loved her.

Viola's heart melted as she listened. "How could any woman refuse such a man?" she wondered.

"Now Cesario, will you go and see Olivia for me?" said the duke at last. "She's bound to listen to you!"

Viola bit her lip and nodded. She thought her heart would break. In just three days, she had fallen in love with Orsino herself.

Chapter 2

Fools and lovers

Olivia's house was in uproar. Her
uncle, Sir Toby, had been making
merry all night with his friends, Sir
Andrew and Feste the jester.

"Olivia is very cross with you all," warned Maria, the maid. "Look out, here she comes with Malvolio, that snobby steward of hers."

"Greetings, lady," said Feste.

But Olivia was in no mood for her jester. "Take away the fool," she sighed.

"Yes – take her away!" cried Feste boldly, pointing at Olivia.

"I said take away the *fool*," snapped Olivia.

"So did I!" said Feste. "Let me explain. Why do you mourn, lady?"

"For my brother's death, fool."

"Is he in Hell, lady?"

"No, he is in Heaven, fool."

"The more fool you, to mourn for your brother being in Heaven!"

Despite herself, Olivia smiled.

Malvolio sniffed disapprovingly.

There was a knock at the door and Malvolio went to answer it.

It was Viola, dressed as Cesario. She bowed to Olivia. "Fair lady, Orsino's heart is like a book..."

"Yes, yes, I've read it," yawned Olivia. "He loves me."

"With thunderous groans and sighs of fire..." insisted Viola.

"But I don't love him," Olivia interrupted, shrugging.

15

"If I were Orsino, I wouldn't give up so easily," said Viola.

"Why, what would you do?" Olivia asked.

"I'd build a willow cabin at your gate, and call upon you every day. I'd sing sad love songs all night, and cry out your name... Oh, you'd have no rest, until you pitied me."

Olivia gazed dreamily at the messenger's pretty face. "Tell Orsino I cannot love him – and then come back, er... to tell me how he takes it!" she added hastily.

After Cesario had left, Olivia couldn't stop thinking about him. "Am I falling in love?" she wondered.

Viola, for her part, was worrying about Olivia. "Poor lady, I think she's fallen for my disguise – while my master adores her, and I love him... What will become of this?"

Oh time, you must untangle this, not I,
It is too hard a knot for me to untie.

Back at Orsino's house, the talk was all about love. "I've been in love too," Viola told the duke.

"What was your loved one like?" he asked.

Viola blushed. "Very like you," she blurted.

Orsino laughed. "If only Olivia shared your taste! But women don't feel things as strongly as us *men*."

"That's not true," said Viola
hotly. "My father's daughter loved
a man, but couldn't tell him — and
her feelings ate away at her, like a
worm in the bud..."

The duke listened thoughtfully.
"This boy really understands love,"
he told himself. "If only I could find
a girl like him."

Chapter 3

Making mischief

Later that night, Sir Toby and Sir
Andrew were in a very jolly mood.
They shouted for Maria to bring
ale and Feste to play a song. Soon
they were singing, loudly and not
very tunefully.

Three merry men be we!

"Are you crazy?" came an angry voice. It was Malvolio in his night gown. "Do you know how late it is?"

"You can't stop us," snorted Toby.

Do you think, because you are virtuous, There shall be no more cakes and ale?

"I'll tell Lady Olivia about this,"
snarled Malvolio, stalking off.
Toby shook a fist after him.

Maria laid a hand on Toby's arm.
"I know how to pay Malvolio back.
I'll fake a love letter from Olivia
and let him find it. He's so vain,
he'll think she's in love with him!"

The next morning, Maria, Toby and Feste hid behind a bush to watch Malvolio.

Malvolio was thinking aloud. "I know Olivia admires me," he muttered. "If she married me, I'd be far richer than Toby."

"The rogue..." spluttered Toby.

"But what's this?" went on Malvolio, spotting the letter.

24

He began to read...

To my beloved M,

I am in love. If you are reading this, don't be afraid. I may be your lady but, when we are married, you will be my lord. Some are born great, some achieve greatness, and some have greatness thrust upon them! So be proud, and put on airs and graces. And don't forget to wear your yellow stockings and cross garters – you know I adore them.

"My lady," exclaimed Malvolio, kissing the letter. "I will!" He was so excited, he didn't hear the giggles coming from the bush.

A loud rat-a-tat sounded on the front door. "Hello, is anyone there?" It was Viola.

"Cesario, is that you?" Olivia heard the voice and came running.

Viola bowed. "Dear lady, I come to tell you of Orsino's love..."

"Stop! I don't want to hear about him. You see, I've realized… I'm in love with *you*, Cesario!"

Viola shook her head. "I swear I'll never marry a woman."

"Think about it anyway," begged Olivia. "And please, come back soon!"

✳ Chapter 4 ✳

Another survivor

Down by the seashore, two men were talking. One was a young sailor named Antonio, and the other was the double of Cesario. It was Viola's twin brother, Sebastian.

"I owe you my life," Sebastian was saying. "If your ship hadn't found me..."

"I'm glad to have helped you,"
replied Antonio. "And I'd come
with you now to see the town, but
I must stay out of sight. My city is
at war with Duke Orsino and I'll
be arrested if I'm found here."

The sailor pulled out a jingling bag. "Here, take my purse in case you need money. You can give it back to me tonight at our inn."

Sebastian hesitated, then accepted gratefully. "Until tonight," he called, as he set off.

Olivia was thinking sadly about Cesario when Malvolio came in.

"Sweet lady, ho ho," he simpered. He waggled a yellow-stockinged, cross-gartered leg at her.

"Malvolio, what's the matter with you?" gasped Olivia.

"Why, nothing," he answered. "These garters are a bit tight, but it doesn't matter if you like them."

31

This is very midsummer madness!

Then he tried to kiss Olivia's
hand. Olivia snatched it away and
ran out of the room – straight into
Maria, Toby and Feste, who had
been listening at the door.

"Go and look after Malvolio," she
told them. "He needs help."

The three plotters nodded, doing their best to look serious.

"We'll send for the doctor. And until he arrives, we'll lock Malvolio in a dark room," promised Toby, his eyes glinting. "For his own safety, of course."

But one prank wasn't enough for Sir Toby. He and Feste were soon plotting another – a duel between Sir Andrew and Cesario. "It should be quite a sight," chuckled Toby. "The two most timid men in Illyria!"

Toby went to find Cesario. "Look out for Sir Andrew," he warned. "He wants to fight a duel with you. He's already killed three men..."

Viola turned pale.

Feste, meanwhile, was talking to
Sir Andrew. "Cesario can't wait to
fight you," said Feste. "He's very
skillful with a sword..."

Sir Andrew trembled.

Toby and Feste were pushing the
reluctant fighters at each other
when the sailor, Antonio, walked
past. As soon as he saw Viola,
he drew his sword and leaped to
defend her.

If this young man has offended you, I will answer for it.

All the noise brought two officers running. They grabbed Antonio. "You're under arrest," they shouted.

Before he was led away, Antonio turned to Viola. "I'm sorry, my friend, but I'll need my purse back."

"What purse?" said Viola. "I can lend you some money, but..."

"You refuse – after all I've done for you!" cried Antonio.

"What? I've never seen you before in my life," exclaimed Viola.

The officers dragged Antonio away, leaving Viola puzzling over his words. "Could it mean... is Sebastian still alive?"

Oh if it prove true,
Tempests are kind,
and salt waves
full of love.

✳ Chapter 5 ✳

More mix-ups

Sebastian wasn't finding the town quite as he'd expected. Strangers kept acting as if they knew him.

"So your name isn't Cesario?" laughed a jester. "No, and I'm not Feste, and this isn't my nose."

"Look, here's a coin," said Sebastian at last. "Now go away!"

But no sooner had one man left than two more appeared – Sir Toby and Sir Andrew.

"Cesario," squealed Sir Andrew. "There's for you!" And he ran at Sebastian, his fists flailing.

Bewildered, Sebastian was forced to defend himself. "There's for you, and there and there!" he cried, beating Sir Andrew back.

Then Toby joined in the fight.

"Stop!" Olivia was flying towards
them. "Are you hurt?" she begged
Sebastian – who shook his head
wordlessly.

"Toby, Andrew, out of my sight!"
she ordered. Then she held out her
hand. "Dear Cesario, let me take
you home."

Sebastian blinked in confusion. "Maybe I'm crazy," he thought. "Or maybe this is a dream." But Olivia was so beautiful and so determined to help, he decided it must be all right.

"I'll come," he agreed.

If it be thus to dream, still let me sleep!

Since Olivia had stopped his fun, Sir Toby went to visit Malvolio. His old enemy was locked up in the cellar, and Feste was taunting him.

"What ho," Feste called out in a strange, gruff voice. "I am Dr. Topaz, come to visit Malvolio the lunatic."

Toby stifled his laughter.

"Dr. Topaz, I'm not a lunatic!" pleaded Malvolio through the door. "I've been tricked and locked up here in darkness."

"There is no darkness but ignorance," the 'doctor' replied solemnly. "You had better stay there until you see the light."

Then Feste began to sing in his own voice. "Hey Robin, jolly Robin..."

"Fool!" cried Malvolio. "Is that you? Please, bring me a pen and paper, so I can write to Olivia."

Sir Toby sighed. "Maybe we should let him write," he told Feste. "I don't want to get into more trouble with Olivia."

Back upstairs, alone in Olivia's
rooms, Sebastian pinched himself.
He could hardly believe it – Olivia
was very beautiful and obviously
a great lady, but they had only
just met and already she wanted to
marry him!

"What should I do?" wondered
Sebastian. "I wish I could ask
Antonio, but I can't find him
anywhere."

Now Olivia was coming back, with a loving smile. "The priest is ready to marry us," she said softly.

Sebastian looked into her shining eyes, drew a deep breath and decided. "I'll do it!"

I'll follow this good man, and go with you,
And having sworn truth, ever will be true.

Chapter 6

Happy ever after

A few hours later, Duke Orsino
and Viola were going to see Olivia.
Outside her house, they bumped
into the officers leading Antonio.

"That's the man who helped me
when I was attacked," cried Viola.

The duke frowned. "I recognize
him. He's an enemy of Illyria!" He
turned to Antonio. "What brings
you here?"

"That boy at your side," replied
Antonio bitterly. "I rescued him
from the sea and risked my life
to help him. We came ashore
yesterday and I lent him my purse."

"But as soon as I was arrested, he
pretended not to know me."

Orsino shook his head. "You're
crazy," he said curtly. "This boy has
been in my service since long before
yesterday."

"Dear Cesario, I left for a moment
and you wandered off," cried Olivia,
dashing out of the house.

She tried to fling her arms
around Viola – who dodged behind
Orsino. "I am Orsino's servant, my
lady, not yours."

"But you are my husband,"
Olivia wailed. "Your place is with
me, not Orsino!"

Orsino's face darkened. *"Husband?"* he growled.

"No, not me," pleaded Viola.

"Don't be afraid," whispered Olivia. "The priest will vouch for us."

"It's true," nodded the old priest, when he came. "They swore everlasting love and exchanged rings, just two hours ago."

The duke looked horrified. "I thought you loved me, but you lied," he told his serving boy. "Go! I never want to see you again."

"My lord, no – " gasped Viola.

Before she could finish, there was a shriek and Sir Andrew appeared.

"A doctor, fetch a doctor! That maniac Cesario has attacked Toby – eek, here he is!" He stared.

"B-but..." stammered Viola.

Sebastian came running after Sir Andrew and knelt before Olivia. "Forgive me, love, for fighting your uncle," he said. "I was defending myself and he isn't badly hurt. Er... why are you staring at me like that?"

"Two of them!" exclaimed the duke, looking from twin to twin.

"Most wonderful," sighed Olivia.

"Sebastian, is that you?" cried Antonio.

"Antonio!" Sebastian grinned at his friend. "I've been so worried."

Antonio pointed at Viola. "So who are *you*?"

Only now did Sebastian turn and see the strangely familiar figure. He stared in wonder.

"I never had a brother," he said
slowly. "But I had a sister who was
lost at sea."

Viola smiled. "I had a brother
who looked just like you. I thought
he was lost too."

"If you were a woman, I'd say
welcome, Viola."

Viola pulled off her cap and let her curls tumble down.

With a shout of joy, Sebastian hugged her. Then he turned to Olivia. "I may not be who you thought," he said. "But it seems to have worked out for the best!"

"Yes, definitely," laughed Olivia, taking his hand.

Orsino turned to Viola. "You once told me you loved me..."

"Yes," breathed Viola.

"For my part, I longed to find a girl like you – and now I have. Viola, will you marry me?"

"Oh yes!" cried Viola, bursting with happiness as she clasped Orsino's hand.

Now you shall be your master's mistress.

"A double wedding party!" said Olivia happily. "We should start planning the celebrations. Malvolio can... oh, but he's ill..."

Feste coughed. "Actually, he's much better and, er, sends you this."

Olivia unfolded the paper Feste handed her...

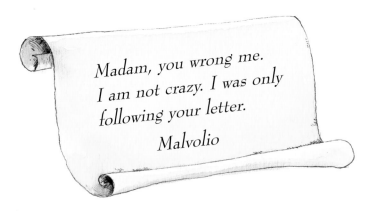

Madam, you wrong me.
I am not crazy. I was only following your letter.
Malvolio

"Bring him here at once!" she said.

Malvolio came, looking pale and angry. He waved the love letter. "Madam, why did you send me this?"

"I never wrote that," said Olivia, startled. "That's not my writing – it's Maria's."

"Don't blame Maria," put in Feste quickly. "Toby and I are just as much at fault. But we shouldn't let old quarrels spoil this happy hour. We have *three* weddings to celebrate, for Toby and Maria are getting married, too."

"Indeed, we should make peace," said the duke. "And to prove it, I forgive Antonio! Now, let's go and plan the celebrations."

Talking excitedly, they all trooped into Olivia's house, until only Feste was left. When he was alone, he began to sing...

A great while ago
the world began
With a hey, ho, the
wind and the rain,
But that's all one,
our play is done,
And we'll strive to
please you every day.

Then, with a bow, he followed the others into the house.

❧ William Shakespeare ❧
1564-1616

William Shakespeare was
born in Stratford-upon-Avon,
England, and became famous
as an actor and writer when he moved to
London. He wrote many poems and almost forty
plays which are still performed and enjoyed today.

❧ Usborne Quicklinks ❧

You can find out more about Shakespeare by
going to the Usborne Quicklinks Website at
www.usborne-quicklinks.com and typing
in the keywords 'yr twelfth night'.
Please note Usborne Publishing cannot be responsible
for the content of any website other than its own.

Designed by Michelle Lawrence
Series designer: Russell Punter
Series editor: Lesley Sims

First published in 2009 by Usborne Publishing Ltd., Usborne House,
83-85 Saffron Hill, London EC1N 8RT, England. www.usborne.com
Copyright © 2009 Usborne Publishing Ltd.